1-1/6/14

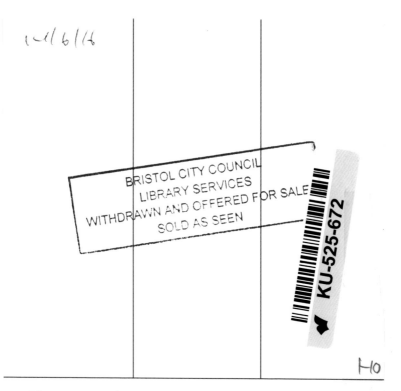

Ho

Please return/renew this item by the last date shown
on this label, or on your self-service receipt.

To renew this item, visit **www.librarieswest.org.uk**
or contact your library.

Your Borrower Number and PIN are required.

LibrariesWest

READZONE

ReadZone Books Limited

2 College Street,
Ludlow,
Shropshire SY8 1AN
www.ReadZoneBooks.com
© in this edition 2015 ReadZone Books Limited

This print edition published in cooperation with Fiction Express, who first published this title in weekly instalments as an interactive e-book.

FICTION EXPRESS

Fiction Express
First Floor Office, 2 College Street,
Ludlow, Shropshire SY8 1AN
www.fictionexpress.co.uk

Find out more about Fiction Express on pages 50-51.

Design: Laura Durman & Keith Williams
Cover Image: Shutterstock Images

© in the text 2015 Simon Cheshire
The moral right of the author has been asserted.

ISBN 978-1-78322-569-9

Printed in Malta by Melita Press.

DEENA'S DREADFUL DAY

SIMON CHESHIRE

What do other readers think?

Here are some comments left on the Fiction Express blog about this book:

"[Deena's Dreadful Day] was brilliant!! A great ending!"
Cherry, Somerset

"I like Deena's Dreadful Day so far. I can't wait until [the next] chapter."
Dylan D, Coventry

" We are really enjoying Deena's Dreadful Day! We like the characters, especially Deena!"
Mrs Moran and Miss Yorke's Year 2 Classes at Allesley Primary School, Coventry

"I'm really enjoying Deena's Dreadful Day"
Adam, Coventry

Contents

Chapter 1

The Big Day

Deena slowly woke up. Her head was under the covers. She did not even want to peep out because it would still be dark and cold outside. She had to get up very early today.

It was Saturday. She was excited. She was also nervous. Today, at 3 o'clock, was the district Young

Talent Contest at the local theatre. Deena was going to perform her magic act. First prize in the contest was a holiday for four people to America.

In her head, she ran through her 'To Do' list. She had a lot to get ready. She had a large bag of props to pack. She had to collect her magician's costume from the shop. She had to be at the theatre by 12:30. She also needed to feed her puppy, Bert, and make sure he was OK. Bert was part of her act. He appeared from a top hat, and he also vanished inside a magic wooden box.

Deena was fully awake now. So much to do! So much to worry about! So much that could go wrong!

Why hadn't her alarm clock gone off? She lifted one eye over the bed covers. It was daylight!

She shot out of bed. She stubbed her toe on her chair. Hopping about, moaning, she searched for her clock.

11:20. She was hours late!

She picked up the clock in horror. She'd forgotten to set the alarm.

With a cry, she raced around her room. She grabbed any clothes she could find. She raced into the bathroom. She raced downstairs, into the kitchen.

"I thought you were getting up early today?" said Deena's mum.

"I meant to!" cried Deena. "I must feed Bert! I must collect my costume before twelve o'clock! I have to be at the theatre by twelve thirty or I might be disqualified! They're very strict about the rules."

Chapter 2

Where's Bert?

"Well I can't drive you," said Mum. "The car's broken down…again."

She had some oily part from the engine on the kitchen table.

"Oh no! I'll have to catch the bus," Deena groaned.

"Why have you got your jumper on inside out?" asked Mum.

"Never mind that now!" gasped

Deena. She quickly tipped dog food in Bert's bowl. She was in such a hurry that she spilt some of it down herself. She hurried over to Bert's bed.

No Bert.

"Where's Bert gone?"

"He was barking for his breakfast," said Mum, poking a screwdriver into the engine part. "Dad fed him."

Deena looked at the bowl of dog food. With a sigh, she left it on the kitchen floor. She hurried into the living room. Dad was reading the newspaper.

"Where's Bert?" asked Deena.

"Why have you got your jeans on back to front?" said Dad.

"Never mind that now!" cried Deena. Suddenly, Bert leapt from behind the sofa. He started sniffing the dog food stains on Deena's jumper. "Stop that!" yelled Deena. "We're very late!"

Deena quickly packed her bag of props. There were her magic wand, playing cards, handkerchiefs, bouncy balls, all sorts of things. She clipped Bert's lead to his collar and they raced out of the house.

A minute later, they were at the bus stop. People kept staring at the dog food stains on Deena's inside-out jumper. Bert kept sniffing them. The bus into town appeared.

Deena looked at her watch. "11:45am. We'll be just in time. The shop is only keeping that costume for me until twelve, and I'll be in trouble if I'm not at the theatre by half past."

Suddenly, icy horror gripped her! She checked her bag. She'd forgotten her best trick, the vanishing box for Bert!

She looked at her phone. The battery had run down. *Now what am I to do?* she thought.

Chapter 3

A Race Against Time

The bus pulled up. People got on and off.

Deena looked at Bert. "What should we do?" she said.

Bert looked up at the bus and barked. "You're right," said Deena. "We'll collect the costume, then return home for the vanishing box. Let's hope we can make it back to the theatre in time!"

They got on to the bus. In town, Deena collected the magician's costume with two minutes to spare! Deena and Bert left the shop, and headed back to the bus stop.

At that moment, Amy Snodgrass hurried past. Amy was Deena's worst enemy from school. She was also her biggest rival in the talent contest!

"Shouldn't you be going *this* way?" said Amy, pointing towards the theatre.

"I'm running late," said Deena through clenched teeth.

"Oh dear," grinned Amy. "I *do* hope you don't get disqualified. Entries close at half past twelve."

"Yes," glared Deena. "I know."

"See you later," smiled Amy, walking on. "Maybe."

Bert growled. He didn't like Amy either.

* * *

Deena and Bert dashed off the bus and raced back home.

"I thought…." came Mum's voice from underneath the car.

"Can't stop!" yelled Deena.

By the time she had collected Bert's vanishing box, and they were back on the bus, it was 12:45.

"We'll only be a little bit late!" sighed Deena. "I hope the judges will let us in." Bert yipped hopefully.

Then the bus took a wrong turn!

Chapter 4

More Disasters

"This isn't the way!" cried Deena.

"Oh no, silly me," said the driver. "Hang on." He stopped the bus and got out a map. The other passengers started to discuss different bus routes.

Deena felt like screaming.

Deena and Bert finally arrived at the theatre at 1:15.

On the big glass entrance door was a sign that said "Talent Contest: Entries Now Open".

"They're running late too! We still have a chance!" cried Deena. At that moment, Amy appeared through the glass door. She turned the sign over. On the back it said "Talent Contest: Entries Closed". Then she noticed Deena. Amy pulled a pretend sad face at her, as if to say "aww, never mind". Then she waved cheerily and locked the door.

"That's it then," sighed Deena. But Bert hadn't given up yet. He raced down an alley at the side of the theatre and began barking.

"An open window!" cried Deena "Good boy – you found a way in!"

Deena clambered through…and fell into a toilet cubicle. As Bert tumbled in, he accidentally pulled the chain. Deena's cloak began to be flushed down the toilet!

Deena quickly pulled the cloak free. It was soaking wet.

Grumbling, Deena marched out of the toilets. Water dripped from her cloak on to the floor. The contestants for the show were gathered. They were listening to the two judges.

Amy spotted Deena as she pushed her way to the front. "Judges!" she called. "That girl there is late. She's sneaked in!"

"I'm sorry," said Deena. "I've had a horrible morning, I got here as fast as I could."

"Sorry, rules are rules," said the lady judge. "Besides, you're all wet. You've got dog food on your jumper."

"B–but the bus took a wrong turn…." explained Deena. "It wasn't really my fault."

"Well, we have still got one spare place," said the man judge, kindly.

"Oh, all right," said the lady judge. "As long as you keep your dog under control." She raised her eyebrows at Bert. The dog had wandered forward and was sniffing her shoe.

"Thank you," said Deena. "I will." She whistled to Bert.

The judges told the contestants to prepare. They had just turned to go, when suddenly Amy kicked the lady judge's ankle.

"Ow!"cried the lady judge. "I think something just bit me!"

"It was that horrid little dog," said Amy, pointing at Bert. "I saw the whole thing."

Chapter 5

Trouble Maker

The lady judge glared at Deena. "You're out of the contest!"

"It wasn't Bert," said Deena.

The man judge scratched his chin. "This is serious. We can't have contestants nibbling at the judges."

"It can't have been Bert," wailed Deena, "He's been sitting here all the time."

The lady judge didn't know who to believe. "I can't prove who's right, so that's that. I'm keeping a sharp eye on you two girls… especially you!" She looked hard at Deena. The judges left the hall. Amy gave Deena a huge, evil grin and skipped away.

Deena and Bert went to the backstage area. All the contestants were practising their acts. There were singers in smart suits. There were twirling dancers. There was a comedian wearing a pair of joke goggle-eyed glasses. A small boy was making colourful balloon animals. They were all very good! Deena felt worried.

She put her cloak on a warm heater to dry. Steam came out of it.

"Where's my lucky baseball cap?" called one of the singers. "Someone has stolen my lucky hat!"

Chapter 6

Smoke and Dust

Two dancers in sparkly costumes approached Deena. "What's your act?" they asked.

"I'm a magician," smiled Deena. She started to unpack the props from her bag. Seeing them made her feel better. She would put on a great show! She was sure she would win!

"Oh dear," said one of the dancers. "No magician has ever won this contest. The lady judge doesn't like magic acts!"

Deena felt worried again. "Never mind," she said bravely. "I'll swirl my cloak and dazzle her with my tricks."

"Cloak?" said the other dancer. "Do you mean that one burning on the heater over there?"

Deena yelped and spun on her heels. The steam rising from the cloak had become smoke!

Bert barked. Deena dashed to the heater and whipped her cloak away.

She flapped it madly. There were scorch marks on it, but it hadn't caught fire.

"I saved it in the nick of time!" Deena told Bert.

At that moment, she noticed something strange. Amy was in the shadows, to one side of the stage. She was whispering something to the lady judge.

"What's Amy up to now?" muttered Deena. She crept closer. She tried to hear what Amy was saying. Her foot caught on an electric cable. The cable pulled tight. There was a mighty WHUMPPHHH!

A large section of glittering scenery came crashing down. A huge cloud of dust covered the stage. Luckily, the scenery didn't fall on anyone!

Everyone turned to stare at Deena. At first, they all looked shocked. Then they began to laugh. Deena's face went red. Meanwhile, Amy had vanished.

Deena helped put the scenery back in place. Then she hurried over to where she'd left her props. "Surely nothing else can go wrong today?" she wailed.

Something else went wrong almost at once.

Chapter 7

Panic!

At that moment, a loud clanging noise echoed through the building. Everyone put their hands to their ears.

The man judge appeared, running up and down and waving his arms about. "Fire!" he yelled. "Fire! Everybody leave by the fire escape!"

"No, it's not a fire," cried Deena. But he wasn't listening.

The contestants all knew what had happened. Deena's smoking cloak had set off the fire alarms. Everyone stared at Deena.

Meanwhile, the man judge was still running up and down. "Fire! Fire! Leave the building!"

"It's just Deena's cloak!" cried the contestants. But he wasn't listening.

Deena checked the time. Less than half an hour until the start of the contest.

"Quick!" she said to Bert. "We've had no time to rehearse. We'd better practise our magic tricks."

At that moment, the theatre doors burst open. Firefighters charged in! They unrolled a long hose.

"Oh no!" cried Deena.

"Fire! Fire!" yelled the man judge.

"No!" cried Deena to the judge. "It was me!"

"It's her!" cried the man judge, pointing at Deena.

"Righto," called a firefighter. He aimed the hose at Deena. WHOOSH! Deena was knocked off her feet by a powerful jet of water.

Chapter 8

Soaked... Again

"Whoops! Sorry," said the firefighter, turning off the hose.

"I was trying to explain...." said Deena. She told them all about her cloak.

The firefighters groaned. Then they rolled up the hose again and left. The man judge mopped his brow with a tissue. "Thank goodness.

The fire's out, everyone! Back to rehearsals! Twenty minutes until curtain up!"

Deena was soaking wet, all over again. "I'd only just dried out," she grumbled. "Oh, this is hopeless! I'm doomed. Today has been one disaster after another. I might as well go home."

Bert whimpered. He looked up at her with sorrowful eyes.

"No, you're right, we'll stay," said Deena. "The show must go on!"

One of the dancers walked by "Have you seen my shoes?" she

asked Deena. Deena replied that she hadn't.

"And the CD with the music for my act," said another dancer. "That's gone too."

Deena turned to Bert. "More things are going missing. Someone's trying to sabotage the contest." Bert nodded his head.

* * *

Outside the theatre, a queue was starting to form at the box office. Lots of people were arriving to see the show.

Backstage, Deena squelched through her magic act with Bert. She was so cold, wet and fed up that she kept forgetting things and getting tricks wrong. She felt very nervous about walking out in front of a big audience!

Meanwhile, several contestants were looking around for their missing hats, shoes, CDs and other items. They were nowhere to be seen!

Amy glided past Deena. "Ewww, you look soggy! What are you? A magical mermaid?" she smiled meanly.

"Places everybody!" called the two judges. "Curtain up in one minute!"

The contestants complained about their missing items, but it was too late now. The show was about to start.

The theatre was packed. The audience hushed. The curtain rose.

Chapter 9

The Cheat

Just then, Deena noticed a figure, in the shadows behind the stage. The figure was carefully taking something from one of the contestants' bags.

"Aha!" thought Deena. "That must be the person who's been trying to ruin the contest! And I'm pretty sure I know who it is!"

She tiptoed up behind the figure, and pounced! She caught…the man judge!

"Well done!" cried the lady judge. She appeared behind Deena, along with Amy. "You've caught him!"

Deena was confused. "What do you mean?"

"This judge's nephew is a contestant – he's the comedian," Amy explained. "We were working out how to catch him ourselves."

"He was trying to spoil the other contestants' acts, so that his nephew would win," said the lady judge.

"I saw you two whispering backstage. I thought you were the ones stealing things," said Deena to Amy and the lady judge. "I'm sorry."

"Hmm," said Amy grandly. "That's alright. But I'm still going to beat you to the prize."

She grinned at Deena as the lady judge hauled the man judge away. He wriggled and grumbled. "Your nephew is disqualified, and so are you!" cried the lady judge.

Chapter 10

Win or Lose?

The audience cheered as the first act took to the stage. It was the singer who'd lost her lucky hat. Now it was safely back on her head!

Only one judge sat at the front now. Deena was very nervous. The lady judge seemed so stern. *And* Deena had accused her of being a thief!

All the acts were good.

Then it was Amy's turn. She was going to recite some poetry.

She walked onto the stage and began reading. She was very good, too. She started reading another poem.

"Thank you Amy. That will do," said the judge. "Next!"

It was Deena's turn. She walked onto the stage with Bert. The audience was hushed. Deena felt very scared. She could see her Mum in the front row. She was still wearing her overalls.

"Here we go!" she whispered
to Bert.

She began her magic act. The
vanishing box trick didn't work –
Bert wouldn't disappear. Every time
she opened the box he was still there!

Deena's card tricks didn't work.
She dropped the cards and they
all got muddled up! Her cloak
got caught on the table and
everything tipped onto the stage!
Her magic wand broke! Every
trick was a disaster!

The audience laughed. The judge
laughed so much she cried.

Deena felt awful. She would *never* win now.

The contest was over. The judge called all the contestants onto the stage.

The audience was excited. The contestants were nervous. Deena was sad and upset.

"I have chosen today's winner," announced the lady judge. For a moment, there was silence. Everyone held their breath. "It's… Deena! That was the funniest act I've seen in years. Your acting was brilliant. It really looked like you were trying to do the tricks correctly. It was so funny when you made them all go wrong. Well done!"

Deena blushed, but said nothing....

The audience cheered! Deena had won!

"We've had a dreadful day," she whispered to Bert, "but at least it ended happily!"

THE END

FICTION EXPRESS

THE READERS TAKE CONTROL!

Have you ever wanted to change the course of a plot, change a character's destiny, tell an author what to write next?

Well, now you can!

'Deena's Dreadful Day' was originally written for the award-winning interactive e-book website Fiction Express.

Fiction Express e-books are published in gripping weekly episodes. At the end of each episode, readers are given voting options to decide where the plot goes next. They vote online and the winning vote is then conveyed to the author who writes the next episode, in real time, according to the readers' most popular choice.

www.fictionexpress.co.uk

WINNER
Education Resources
Award for Innovation

FICTI●N
EXPRESS

TALK TO THE AUTHORS

The Fiction Express website features a blog where readers can interact with the authors while they are writing. An exciting and unique opportunity!

FANTASTIC TEACHER RESOURCES

Each weekly Fiction Express episode comes with a PDF of teacher resources packed with ideas to extend the text.

"The teaching resources are fab and easily fill a whole week of literacy lessons!"
Rachel Humphries, teacher at Westacre Middle School

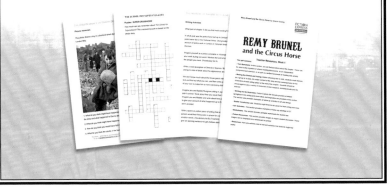

FICTION EXPRESS

The Sand Witch
by Tommy Donbavand

When twins Chris and Ella are left to look after their younger brother on a deserted beach, they expect everything to be normal, boring in fact. But then something extraordinary happens! Will the Sand Witch succeed in passing on her sandy curse in this exciting adventure?

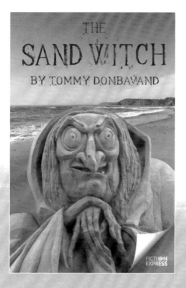

ISBN 978-1-78322-544-6

FICTI●N EXPRESS

The Rise of the Rabbits
by Barry Hutchison

When twins Harvey and Lola are given the school rabbit, Mr Lugs, to look after for the weekend, they're both very excited. That is until the rabbit begins to mutate and decides the time has come for bunnies to rise up and seize control.

It's up to Harvey and Lola to find a way to return Mr Lugs and his friends to normal, before the menaces sweep across the country – and then the world!

ISBN 978-1-78322-540-8

FICTION EXPRESS

Snaffles the Cat Burglar
by Cavan Scott

When notorious feline felon Snaffles and his dim canine
sidekick Bonehead are caught red-pawed trying to steal
the Sensational Salmon of Sumatra, not everything is what
it seems. Their capture leads them on a top-secret mission
for the Ministry of Secret Shenanigans.

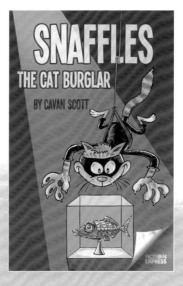

ISBN 978-1-78322-543-9

FICTION EXPRESS

The Vampire Quest
by Simon Cheshire

James is an ordinary boy, but his best friend Vince is a bit... odd. For one thing, it turns out that Vince is a vampire. His parents are vampires, too. And so are the people who live at No. 38. There are vampires all over the place, it seems, but there's nothing to worry about. They like humans, and they'd never, ever do anything...horrible to them. Unless... the world runs out of Feed-N-Gulp, the magical vegetarian vampire brew. Which is exactly what's just happened....

ISBN 978-1-78322-553-8

Simon Cheshire

Simon Cheshire is an award-winning children's writer who has been visiting schools, libraries and literary festivals for well over a decade. He's done promotional book tours around various parts of the UK and America, he's written and presented a number of radio programmes, but he has yet to achieve his ambition of going to the Moon.

Simon was a dedicated reader from a very young age, and started writing stories when he was in his teens. After he turned thirty and finally accepted he'd always have the mind of a ten-year-old, he began creating children's stories and at last found his natural habitat. Since his first book appeared in 1997, his work has been published in various countries and languages around the world.

He's written for a broad range of ages, but the majority of his work is what he calls "action-packed comedies" for 8-12 year olds. He lives in Warwick with his wife and children, but spends most of his time in a world of his own.